Words of
LOVE

JAKE BIGGIN

These Words of Love belong to:

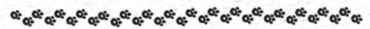

Little people
or big people—
all of us have questions.
We have worries.
We have doubts.
We feel lonely sometimes.
Sometimes we just
need someone to listen.

Wise Little Dog Sunny
has little thoughts about big questions.
He's smart and full of love.
He's a loyal companion, guide, and mentor.
He's who we'd like to think that we sometimes are.

Sunny is simply... a friend.

Hello, Alice.
I'm Sunny.

Can we be best friends?

But I don't know how to make friends.

I do.

I have so many questions...

Ask me. I might be able to help.
Or at the very least, I can listen.

Where do I start?

Just try to be honest
about how you feel.

I have some of my best
thoughts when I'm out walking.
Should we go on an adventure?

You're not messing up—
you're learning.

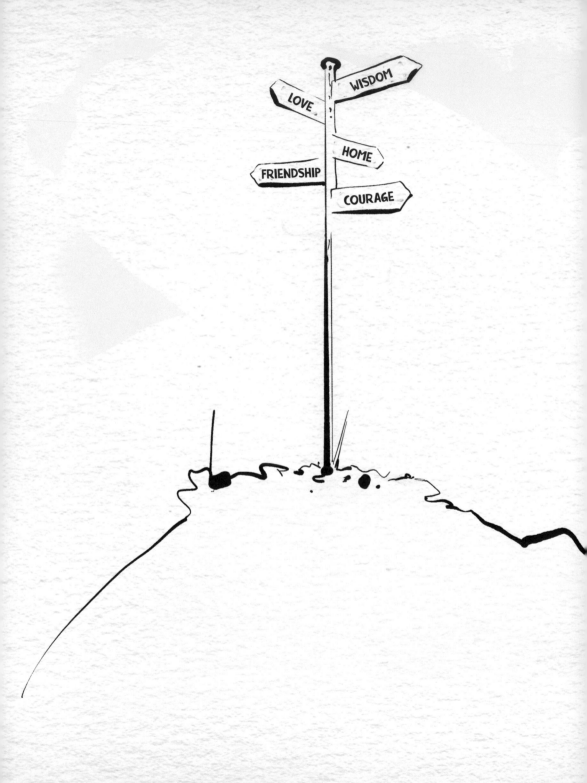

Which way should we go?

Sometimes we just need to choose
one path and see where it leads.

I sometimes feel silly if I have to ask for help.

No one makes it on their own.
We all need help now and then.

What if I don't know where to start?

Why not pick just one small thing
and start from there?

Does everything change?

Most things do.
But change can be beautiful.

Don't worry about things
that haven't happened yet.

Happiness can always be found.
Let's look for it together.

What's the difference between
liking and loving something?

If you like a flower, you pick it.
But if you love a flower,
you water it every day.

What do you love about me?

Your kind heart.

Who make the best friends?

People who want the best for you.

How can I be a good friend?

Listening is good...

Make everybody...

feel like a somebody.

Wherever you go...

go with all your heart in
the direction of your dreams.

What if I don't get there?

Don't give up. You may
have to cross the same river
more times than you think.

Being different just
means you're brave
enough to be yourself.

You are enough.

Don't be afraid to use your voice.

You can always
tell me how you feel...

even if you're scared to.

What does friendship mean?

I think friendship is
another word for love.

Friendship means
you are never alone.

Saying goodbye makes me sad.

Me too. But how lucky we are to have someone we don't want to say goodbye to.

I will stay with you.

I see you.

I hear you.

You are loved.

Sometimes there are no words.

But I'm here.

What do YOU love?

Watching you grow.

Thank you, Sunny.

Author and Illustrator Jake Biggin

Editor Rona Skene
Senior Art Editor Rachael Parfitt Hunt
US Senior Editor Shannon Beatty
Additional Editorial Work Becca Arlington
Senior Production Editor Nikoleta Parasaki
Production Controller Magdalena Bojko
Jacket Coordinator Magda Pszuk
Deputy Art Director Mabel Chan
Publisher Francesca Young
Publishing Director Sarah Larter

First American Edition, 2023
Published in the United States by DK Publishing
1745 Broadway, 20th Floor, New York, NY 10019

DK, a Division of Penguin Random House LLC
24 25 26 27 28 10 9 8 7 6 5 4 3 2 1
001–338292–August/2024

ISBN: 978-0-7440-9847-1

Printed and bound in China

www.dk.com

MIX
Paper | Supporting
responsible forestry
FSC™ C018179

This book was made with Forest
Stewardship Council™ certified
paper – one small step in DK's
commitment to a sustainable future.
**For more information go to
www.dk.com/our-green-pledge**

For Sam and Alice